W9-AHK-037

NEUGEBAUER PRESS USA

SANTA'S
FAVORITE
Hisako Aoki
Ivan Gantschev
STORY

One cold day in December a fox was walking in the forest. As he looked at the snowy trees, he remembered that it would soon be Christmas. Then he heard something. He sniffed the air and looked around.

There, fast asleep against a tree, was Santa Claus! He was snoring.
"Oh my goodness!" thought the fox, "Santa Claus has come early
this year. I'd better go and tell everyone he's here."
So he hurried off to tell all the other animals that lived in the forest.

When they heard the news, the animals hopped and ran and scampered and flew to the tree. A squirrel chattered excitedly, and Santa Claus slowly stretched, yawned, and then opened his eyes to see the faces of a dozen little creatures.

"Why are you here?" they asked him.

"Is Christmas going to be early this year?" asked the fox.

"I'm sorry if I've worried you, my friends," said Santa. "I went for a long hike this morning to get in shape for Christmas Eve, but I guess I walked until I got too tired. Maybe all those heavy presents will be too much for me to deliver this year."

The animals looked alarmed.

"Does that mean there won't be a Christmas anymore?" asked the fox.

"No, no, no," said Santa in a kindly voice, "Christmas hasn't got anything to do with me. Sit down and I'll tell you all the story of the first Christmas."

"It happened long, long ago in a faraway place called Bethlehem. Some shepherds were watching over their sheep in the fields outside the town. It was very quiet and still."

"Suddenly a beautiful bright star appeared in the sky. The shepherds heard a voice saying, 'Do not be afraid. I have good news for you all. Today in the town of Bethlehem, the Christ Child has been born. God has sent His Son to show what God's love is like. Follow the star to his stable.'"

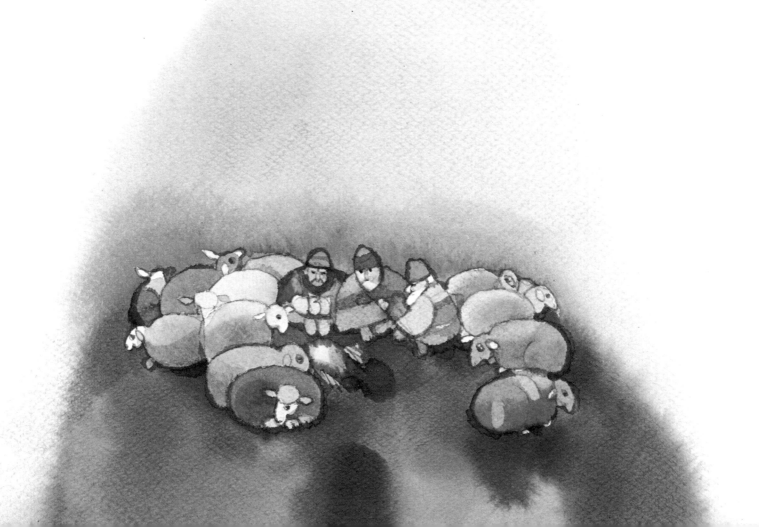

"The shepherds followed the star over hills and through valleys, across bridges and past little villages."

"All the while the star shone brighter and brighter until at last it stopped above a small stable. The shepherds and their sheep stopped too, for there in the stable was a baby, lying in a manger. The shepherds knew that this was the Son of God, and they knelt down and prayed."

"And that is what happened in Bethlehem when the Christ child came. It's my favorite story because it reminds me why we are so happy at this time of year. Love was the gift God gave to us on the first Christmas, and it still is, you know. And this love is far better than any presents I can ever deliver." Santa Claus put his hands in his pockets and looked slowly around the circle of animals with a kind and happy smile upon his face.

"How silly we have been," said the fox, "to think that Christmas was only about presents."

"So now you know!" said Santa. "But come on—you're right that it's almost Christmas. Let's go back to my place and get things ready." All the animals followed as Santa Claus ran off toward his house. He didn't even look tired any more, because he had remembered how much fun his work was going to be.

The animals stayed at Santa's house until Christmas Day, and helped him every way they could. Of course, the reindeer helped by going out with him to deliver the presents the night before. After a fine Christmas dinner, Santa gave every animal a present. And as they sat around the fireplace later in the day, they all asked to hear Santa's favorite story again. It was a very special Christmas Day for everyone.

Santa was sure that he had the nicest time of all, though, because he remembered that the best present ever is Christmas itself.